This
Korky Paul
PICTURE BOOK
BELONGS TO:

_____

_____

Endpapers by Jeffrey Tan aged 8.
Thank you to Wolvercote Primary School, Oxford for helping with the endpapers.

To Deb, Bosh and Poppy – J.L.
To Sarah Stoffer – K.P.

OXFORD
UNIVERSITY PRESS

Great Clarendon Street, Oxford OX2 6DP
Oxford University Press is a department of the University of Oxford.
It furthers the University's objective of excellence in research, scholarship,
and education by publishing worldwide in

Oxford New York

Auckland Cape Town Dar es Salaam Hong Kong Karachi
Kuala Lumpur Madrid Melbourne Mexico City Nairobi
New Delhi Shanghai Taipei Toronto

With offices in

Argentina Austria Brazil Chile Czech Republic France Greece
Guatemala Hungary Italy Japan Poland Portugal Singapore
South Korea Switzerland Thailand Turkey Ukraine Vietnam

Oxford is a registered trade mark of Oxford University Press
in the UK and in certain other countries

Originally published as *The Cat That Scratched* by The Bodley Head Children's Books 1994
First published by Oxford University Press 2009

2 4 6 8 10 9 7 5 3 1

British Library Cataloguing in Publication Data
Data available

ISBN: 978-0-19-272900-2 (paperback)

Printed in China

Paper used in the production of this book is a natural,
recyclable product made from wood grown in sustainable forests.
The manufacturing process conforms to the environmental
regulations of the country of origin.

www.korkypaul.com

A Cat Called Scratch

Written by Jonathan Long

OXFORD

UNIVERSITY PRESS

Scratch the cat had a terrible itch.
A flea in his fur was making him twitch.

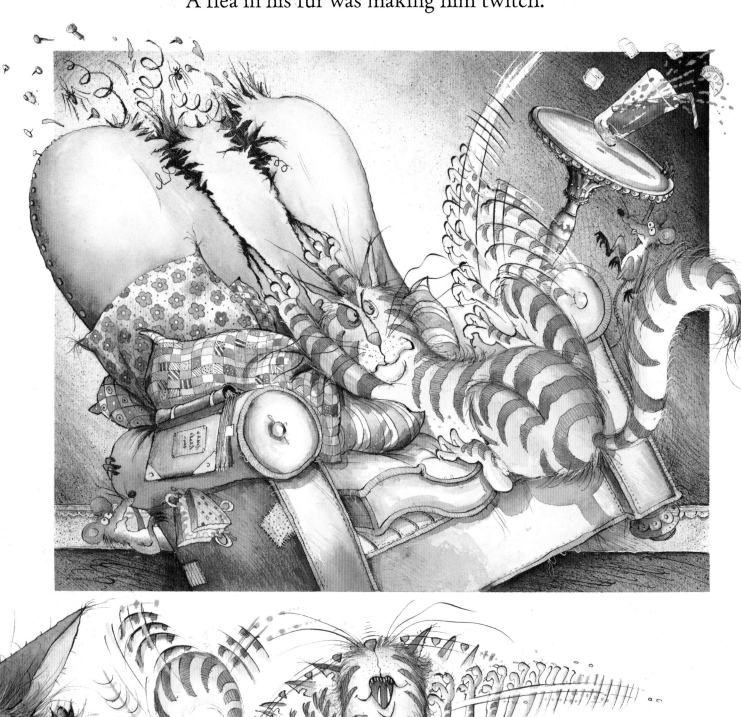

He scratched himself here and scritched himself there.
He scritched upside down and scratched in mid-air.

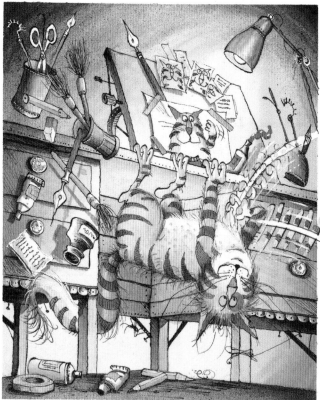

He whirled his paws madly and span like a top,
Fell head over heels, and then rolled to a stop.

'Ha ha!' said a voice, all tiny and teasy.
'To get rid of *me* won't be nearly that easy!'

'Oh really?' said Scratch. 'You bothersome bug!
When I've finished with you, you won't sound so smug.'

SCRITCH
SCRATCH SCRATCH
SCRITCH SCRATCH SCRATCH
SCRITCH
SCRATCH SCRATCH
SCRATCH

He went to the cupboard, opened the door,
And dragged out the hoover onto the floor.

He plugged in the plug and flicked on the switch,
And said, 'Time to go, you tortuous titch.'

He hoovered his tummy, his ears and his nose,
And each of his legs, right down to his toes.

But catastrophe struck — his tail was sucked in,
And the hoover blew up with a deafening din.

Scratch opened his eyes — he was stuck to the rafter
But still he could hear that pesky flea's laughter.

'Ha ha!' said a voice, all tiny and teasy.
'To get rid of *me* won't be nearly that easy!'

'You nigglesome nit, you mischievous mite!
I'm mad now,' said Scratch, 'and ready to fight!'

He ran down the road to a friendly hairdresser
Who wore a pink gown and was called 'Trendy Tessa.

'I need you,' said Scratch, 'to keep this hush-hush:
A flea's in my fur and I'd like a good brush.'

Tess groomed him all over with brushes and combs,
Curled him, and clipped him, and sprayed him with foam.

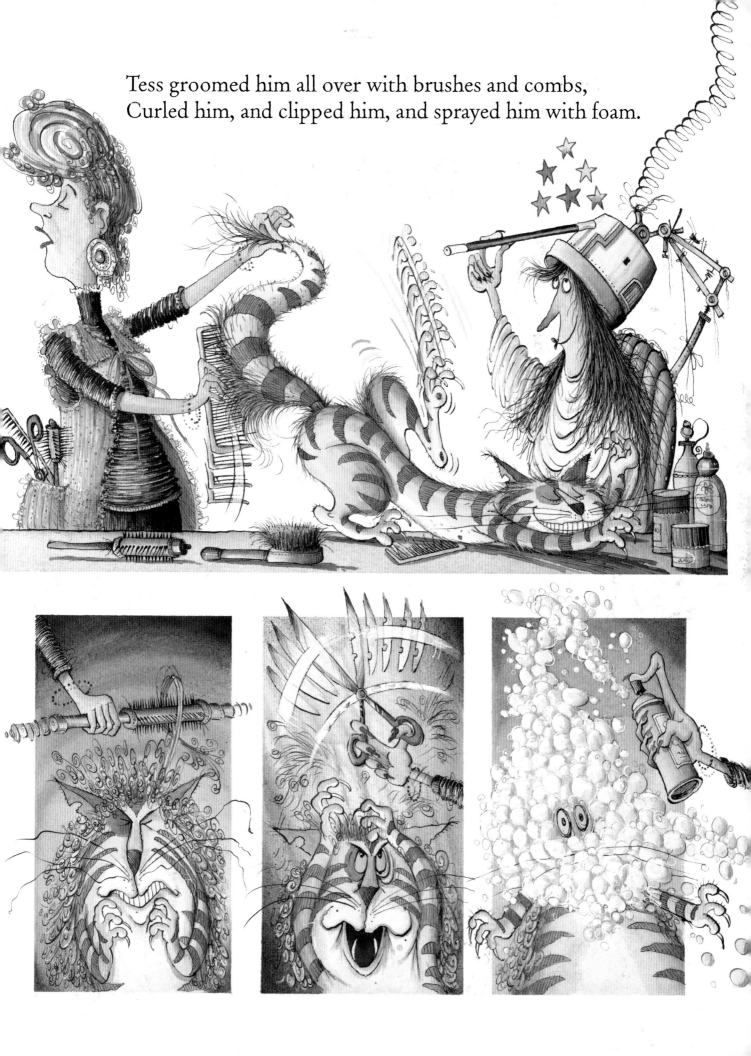

But when it was done the poor cat looked a fright,
And — can you believe it? — he felt something *bite*!

'Ha ha!' said a voice, all tiny and teasy.
'To get rid of *me* won't be nearly that easy!'

'Lousiest louse! Pernickety pest!
It's time I put you to the ultimate test.'

Scratch dashed to the carwash and paid 50p
To the cheerful attendant drinking his tea.

He dived right inside the largest of washers
With rollers and soapers and powerful sploshers.

Scrub-a-dub-dub, it went, dub-a-scrub-scrub,
And rolled him around like a sock in a tub.

But he swallowed some water which made him feel groggy
And he had to get out, the poor waterlogged moggy!

'Ha ha!' said a voice, all tiny and teasy.
'To get rid of *me* won't be nearly that easy!'

'Oh no!' wailed the cat, feeling awfully poorly,
'It looks like I'm stuck with this creepiest crawly!'

But just then he heard shouts and a hullabaloo:
A rather large lion had escaped from the zoo.

The lion gave Scratch a big friendly smile
And asked for a place he might hide for a while.

Before Scratch could answer, he heard a small pop,
His flea had moved on with a jump and a hop.

But the lion was quick — with a pat of his paw
The flea was flicked and trapped under his claw.

'Grrr,' said the lion, 'that flea made a bungle,
He shouldn't have messed with the King of the Jungle!'

'Oh, thank you!' said Scratch, 'for sorting that flea.
Would you like to come home and stay with me?'

He said to the lion, 'My home is now yours.'
Then they fixed up a sign before going indoors.

They fell fast asleep, with their tails gently curled
The happiest cats in the whole of the world.